HEINEMA
INTE

PHILIP PROWSE

Bristol Murder

HEINEMANN ELT

INTERMEDIATE LEVEL

Series Editor: John Milne

The Heinemann Guided Readers provide a choice of enjoyable reading material for learners of English. The series is published at five levels – Starter, Beginner, Elementary, Intermediate and Upper. At **Intermediate Level**, the control of content and language has the following main features:

Information Control

Information which is vital to the understanding of the story is presented in an easily assimilated manner and is repeated when necessary. Difficult allusion and metaphor are avoided and cultural backgrounds are made explicit.

Structure Control

Most of the structures used in the Readers will be familiar to students who have completed an elementary course of English. Other grammatical features may occur, but their use is made clear through context and reinforcement. This ensures that the reading, as well as being enjoyable, provides a continual learning situation for the students. Sentences are limited in most cases to a maximum of three clauses and within sentences there is a balanced use of simple adverbial and adjectival phrases. Great care is taken with pronoun reference.

Vocabulary Control

There is a basic vocabulary of approximately 1,600 words. Help is given to the students in the form of illustrations which are closely related to the text.

Glossary

Some difficult words and phrases in this book are important for understanding the story. Some of these words are explained in the story, some are shown in the pictures, and others are marked with a number like this ...[3] Words with a number are explained in the Glossary on page 77.

Contents

The People in This Story

Name: Peter Jones

Age: 22

Address: 103 Mill Road, Bridgwater.

Description: tall, thin, dark hair, brown eyes.

Life: Peter Jones was fifteen when his father died. Peter's mother was very poor and needed money, so Peter got a job. Peter gave all the money he earned to his mother to help pay for the house where they lived. Their house was very small and old but it was cheap. When he was seventeen, Peter changed his job and started to work for a company called Universal Transport Limited. This company had a lot of lorries. As soon as he was old enough, Peter learnt to drive. When he was twenty-one, he passed a driving test[1] which allowed him to drive big lorries on his own. Now he drives lorries with goods[2] in them from Bridgwater to Bristol, London, Birmingham and Manchester.

Name: John Stevens

Age: 16

Address: 24 Devonshire Road, Bristol.

Description: medium height, thin, brown hair, brown eyes.

Life: John Stevens' mother and father are dead. He lives with his uncle. His uncle, Robert Stevens, is a school teacher. John is still at school but he doesn't enjoy it and he wants to leave.

Name: Jeff Beck

Age: 24

Address: Cabaret Club, 12 Victoria Street, Manchester.

Description: medium height, quite fat, long dark hair, blue eyes.

Life: Jeff Beck left school at fifteen. He was soon in trouble with the police. When he was eighteen, he was sent to prison for three months for stealing cars. After he left prison, he continued stealing and was caught again. He is now twenty-four and has been in prison three times. He is the owner of a night club[3].

Name: Bob Steel

Age: 42

Address: 12 River Street, Bristol.

Description: short, average weight, red hair, small red beard, green eyes.

Life: Nothing is known about his childhood. He has no job. He sells information to the police about robberies and people who steal.

1

Early Morning

It was early one morning in October. Mrs Jones was in the kitchen making breakfast. She had been up since five o'clock. Mrs Jones looked at her watch. It was time to wake Peter.

'Peter, Peter. It's six o'clock. Get up!' she shouted up the stairs. Peter was already awake.

'What?' he asked.

'It's six o'clock,' his mother shouted.

'Oh, OK[4],' Peter replied. He could smell the breakfast which his mother had prepared for him. He got out of bed slowly and went to the bathroom.

'Peter!' his mother shouted again.

'Yes, Mum. It's OK. I'm up,' Peter shouted back through the door. He washed quickly because it was cold and ran back to his bedroom.

'Peter. Your breakfast's ready,' Mrs Jones continued.

'Yes, Mum. I'm coming,' Peter replied as he was dressing. He ran down the stairs and went through the sitting room to the kitchen.

'Oh, here you are,' his mother said. 'Hurry up or your breakfast will go cold.' Peter sat down and ate his breakfast.

'Do you want some more tea?' Peter's mother asked.

'Yes, please,' Peter replied, with a smile.

'Where are you going today?' Mrs Jones asked, as she was pouring out the tea.

'I don't know,' Peter said. 'What's the time?'

'It's half past six,' answered Mrs Jones, looking at her watch.

'I must go,' Peter said, finishing his cup of tea. 'Thanks for breakfast.'

'What time will you come back this evening?' asked Mrs Jones anxiously.

Peter stood up. 'I don't know. If it's a long drive, I won't be back until tomorrow.'

'Take care of yourself[5], Peter,' his mother said, giving him his coat.

'Don't worry, Mum, I will,' said Peter. Then he quickly put his coat on and went out into the hall.

'Goodbye,' his mother shouted.

'See you, Mum.' He went out of the front door into the street. He walked along to the end of the street and turned right. As he turned the corner, he saw the bus and started to run. He ran as fast as he could and got on the bus just before it left.

'Corporation Street, please,' he said to the driver.

'Fifty pence, please,' replied the driver.

Peter paid and sat down. The bus drove quickly through the empty streets and was soon in Corporation Street. Peter got off and walked along the street to Universal Transport Ltd. He went through the gate and into the office.

'Good morning, Mr James,' said Peter cheerfully, as he entered the office.

'Good morning, Peter. How are you?' said Mr James looking up from his desk. Mr James decided where the lorries went every day and gave the drivers their instructions. He was a short, fat man, aged about forty-five. He was popular with the drivers because he had been a driver himself once. So Mr James understood the drivers' problems.

'I'm fine, thanks,' replied Peter.

'Good,' said Mr James, 'I want you to take a load[6] of biscuits to Manchester today. You can stay the night there and come back tomorrow.'

'Right,' answered Peter. 'Is the lorry ready?'

'No, Peter, not yet. Can you help load[7] it, please?' asked Mr James.

Peter went outside and walked over to his lorry. He helped put the boxes of biscuits in the lorry and then drove it to the gate. The man at the gate gave Peter the address for the biscuits in Manchester and asked Peter to sign some papers. Peter thanked him, got back into the lorry and drove out of the gate.

It was still only half past seven and Bridgwater was quiet. He drove along Corporation Street and through the centre of the town. The town was empty and all the shops were still closed. Peter drove on and soon passed people leaving their houses and hurrying to work. Peter took the road for Bristol and by eight o'clock he had left Bridgwater and was out in the country. He turned on the radio and listened:

'It will be cold in most of England today, and there will probably be heavy rain. That is the end of the weather forecast[8]. Now it is eight o'clock and time for the news. . . . A middle-aged man was murdered in Bristol late last night. The police would like to talk to a boy of about sixteen who . . .'

Peter turned off the radio. He was always unlucky. Today he had to drive all the way to Manchester and it was going to rain. As he was thinking about the weather the first few drops of rain started to fall.

It was still raining when Peter reached Bristol. It was after nine o'clock now and all the shops were open. There were lots of people and cars and he had to drive slowly. He took the road to the north and was through the town in half an hour. Not bad, he thought. I'll get to Birmingham by lunchtime.

As Peter looked out ahead, he saw a boy standing by the side of the road. It was difficult to see in the rain but the boy looked about sixteen. He was wearing a red jersey, and jeans. He was hitch-hiking[9] and was holding out his hand to ask for a lift[10].

Peter got back into the lorry and drove out of the gate.

Peter slowed down and stopped. The boy ran up and opened the door.

'Where are you going?' the boy asked.

'Manchester,' Peter said.

'Can you give me a lift?' the boy asked anxiously.

'Yes, get in.' As he spoke, Peter leant over and helped the boy into the lorry. The boy closed the door. He was very, very wet. Peter drove off.

'Where are you going?' asked Peter.

'I don't know,' said the boy.

'You don't know?' Peter repeated, in a surprised voice.

'No. I've run away from home.' The boy spoke quietly.

'What?' said Peter. The lorry was very noisy and it was difficult to talk.

'I said I've run away from home.' The boy repeated his words loudly but Peter still could not hear.

'What?' Peter asked again.

'I said I've left home. I'm not going to go back,' the boy shouted.

'Why?' asked Peter.

'We had an argument, that's all,' the boy replied slowly.

'What's your name?' inquired Peter.

'John. John Stevens. What's yours?' the boy asked.

'Peter,' replied the lorry driver. 'Well, John, do you feel like a cup of tea?'

'Yes, please.' The boy smiled with pleasure at the idea of a cup of tea.

'There's a café just ahead and we'll stop there,' said Peter, pointing in the direction of the café as he spoke. The lorry stopped outside the café. It was still raining heavily and John and Peter ran inside.

Peter slowed down and stopped.

2

The Newspaper

It was warm in the café and Peter went up to the counter where a girl was serving. John took a seat at a table.

'Two teas, please,' said Peter to the girl at the counter.

'Here you are, love,' said the girl, as she pushed two cups of tea towards Peter. 'That's ninety pence, please.'

Peter gave her the money and carried the cups of tea over to the table where John was sitting.

'Thank you,' said John. The tea was hot and sweet and warmed both of them up.

'So you've left home, then,' said Peter.

'That's right,' John replied.

'Why?' Peter asked.

'I told you. We had an argument,' said the boy.

Peter smiled. 'You don't have to tell me if you don't want to.'

'I want to,' said John. 'I must talk to someone.'

'Tell me what happened then,' said Peter, in a kind voice.

'Well, you see,' John began, 'my parents are dead and I live with my uncle.'

Peter interrupted the boy. 'In Bristol?'

'Yes, that's right,' said John. 'My uncle has always been kind to me, but he never lets me do anything.'

'What do you mean?' asked Peter.

The boy pushed back his chair. 'Well, he never lets me go out in the evenings.'

Peter nodded. 'Why not?'

'Oh,' the boy said, 'he says that I must stay in and study instead. He makes me stay in and study every night while my friends are out enjoying themselves.'

'I see,' said Peter, as he drank his tea. 'That's why you ran away, is it?'

John shook his head. 'Not really. It was because of what happened last night.'

'What did happen?' asked Peter, watching the boy's face closely.

'I told my uncle that I wanted to go to the cinema with some of my friends,' John explained, 'but my uncle wouldn't let me go and told me to study instead.'

'Yes,' said Peter, encouraging the boy to continue his story.

'When he wasn't looking, I ran out and went to the cinema with my friends. When I came back my uncle was waiting for me. He was very, very angry and asked me where I had been. I told him I'd been to the cinema. When I told him that I'd been to the cinema, my uncle hit me in the face.' John paused to drink his tea.

'Does he often hit you?' asked Peter.

'When he gets angry. Last night he hit me very hard and I got angry and hit him back,' replied John.

Peter's face was serious. 'What did your uncle do then?' he asked.

'Nothing. You see I must have hit him very hard because he fell on the floor and didn't move.' John stopped speaking and looked at the table.

'What did you do then?' asked Peter quietly.

'I was . . .,' John hesitated, 'I was afraid and so I ran out.'

'Where did you go?' inquired Peter.

'I can't remember. When I came back an hour later, there were several police cars outside the house. All the lights in the house were switched on. Then a policeman came out of the house and saw me. "There he is," he shouted and ran after me. I ran away and the policeman didn't catch me. I slept in the bus station and started hitch-hiking early this morning.'

14

'Well,' said Peter, 'you certainly had a busy night. Why did you run away from the police?'

'Because they wanted to catch me and put me in prison,' answered John.

'But why do you think they wanted to put you in prison?' continued Peter.

'Because my uncle must have telephoned the police. He must have told them to catch me because I had hit him.'

'Do you want some more tea?' asked Peter.

John nodded. 'Yes, please.'

'Here's ninety pence,' said Peter handing John the money. 'Can you go and get two more teas?'

John went to get the tea. There were a lot of people in the café and he had to wait. Peter picked up a newspaper which someone had left on the table.

Peter looked at the front page:

Man Found Dead

The body of Mr Robert Stevens, 44, was found in his home at 24 Devonshire Road, Bristol last night.

There must have been a fight because a lot of the furniture was broken. Nothing has been stolen.

Police are looking for Mr Stevens' nephew, John Stevens, aged 16, who lived with him.

When Peter had read this, he quickly put the newspaper in his pocket. A minute later John returned with the tea.

'Was there anything interesting in the paper?' John asked.

'No,' said Peter. 'Drink up your tea because we must leave as soon as possible.' They finished their tea quickly and walked out to the lorry. Peter started the engine and drove off. It had stopped raining and the sun was shining. It was now warm inside the lorry and John began to feel sleepy.

'If you want to sleep,' Peter said, 'you can get into the back.

The lorry's not quite full and there's an old coat of mine there you can lie on.'

'Thanks,' said John, 'that would be good.'

Peter stopped the lorry and John got into the back. They drove off again. Peter drove as fast as he could in order to make up for lost time. There were only a few cars and soon the lorry was near Tewkesbury. Suddenly Peter saw a police car stopped on the road ahead. As he drove closer, a policeman walked out in front of the lorry and held his hand up.

3

The Lorry is Stopped

The policeman held his hand up. Peter slowed the lorry down and stopped. The policeman walked up to the side window.

'What is it?' asked Peter. 'What's the matter?'

'We're looking for a boy who we think may have killed his uncle,' replied the policeman.

'Oh, yes,' said Peter, 'I heard the news about it on the radio this morning.'

'Well,' continued the policeman, 'we think the boy has left Bristol and he may be hitch-hiking north.'

'Is he dangerous?' asked Peter.

'Very dangerous. He killed his uncle with a chair leg,' the policeman added.

'What does he look like?' asked Peter.

The policeman took out his notebook and read, 'John Stevens, aged 16. Brown hair. Brown eyes. Average height. Last seen wearing a red jersey and blue jeans.' The policeman looked up from his book. 'Have you seen him?' he asked Peter.

'Yes,' said Peter, 'I've seen hundreds of young men dressed

like that this morning. It could have been any of them.'

'OK,' said the policeman, 'thanks for your help. If you do see him let us know, won't you?'

'Of course,' replied Peter and started the engine.

'Cheerio,' shouted the policeman.

'Just a minute,' said another voice. The policeman turned around. Another policeman was getting out of the police car. He was big and red-faced and had a nasty voice.

'What is it now?' asked Peter. 'I've got to be in Manchester before five o'clock.'

'All right. This won't take long,' said the second policeman. 'We're going to search your lorry.'

'Why?' asked Peter angrily.

'The boy may be hiding there.' Both policemen walked around to the back of the lorry.

What shall I do now, thought Peter. I could drive off before they look in the back. But if I do drive away they'll drive after me and their car is much faster than my lorry. What shall I do? Sit here and wait. If they find John, I can say that I didn't know he was in my lorry.

'Hey, you!' shouted one of the policemen.

They've found him, thought Peter.

'Hey, you, come and help us open the back of your lorry.'

'Right,' shouted Peter and got out. If I'm there when they find John, he thought, perhaps I can give him a chance to escape by getting in the policemen's way. Peter walked around to the back of the lorry and opened it for the policemen. They looked in. All they could see was a lot of boxes and, in one corner, some old coats on the floor.

'Right,' said the second policeman, 'I'm sorry to have made you wait so long. You can go now.'

Peter thanked him, got into the lorry and drove off. He drove for ten minutes until he was sure that the police car was not following him. Then he stopped, jumped out and ran around to

All they could see was a lot of boxes and, in one corner,
some old coats on the floor.

the back of the lorry. He opened it and looked in. He couldn't see John anywhere. Peter climbed into the back. He couldn't understand where John was. The old coat was there but John wasn't lying on it. Then Peter saw something that the police hadn't noticed. He could see part of a shoe sticking out from under the coat. Peter smiled when he thought how stupid the police were not to have looked under the coat. He went up to the coat and said loudly: 'This is the police. Come out at once. We know you are under the coat.'

'All right,' said a voice from under the coat, and John slowly got up.

'Oh, it's you,' said John. 'I thought you were the police.'

'No,' replied Peter. 'I was just playing a joke on you.'

'You did frighten me,' said John. 'I had a strange dream when I was asleep.'

'What!' exclaimed Peter. 'Have you been asleep all the time?'

'Yes, I dreamt the police were searching the lorry.'

'That wasn't a dream,' replied Peter. 'It was real.'

'You mean that the police stopped the lorry when I was asleep?' asked John.

Peter nodded his head. 'Yes,' he said.

'And you didn't tell them where I was?' asked John.

'No,' said Peter.

'But why did you help me?' asked John. 'You could have got into trouble yourself.'

'Because I don't think you did what the police said,' answered Peter.

'What has my uncle told them?' asked John.

'Your uncle hasn't told them anything.'

'Well, in that case . . .' said John.

'Because he's dead,' said Peter quietly.

'Oh, no,' cried John. 'I didn't hit him very hard.'

'If you hit someone with a chair leg,' continued Peter, 'you don't have to hit them very hard to kill them.'

'A chair leg?' replied John in surprise. 'I didn't hit him with a chair leg. I hit him with my hands.'

Peter took the newspaper out of his pocket and showed John the article about the murder.

'Are you sure?' asked Peter.

'Yes,' said John firmly.

'Then I was right not to tell the police about you,' said Peter. 'We'd better start again now or else we'll never get to Manchester, or find out who killed your uncle.'

4

Arriving in Manchester

By five o'clock Peter and John were outside Manchester.

'Have you ever been here before?' asked Peter.

'No, I haven't,' said John.

'Well, this is what we'll do. I've got to take my load of biscuits to this address.' He gave John a piece of paper. 'It'll take me an hour or two to unload everything and then I'm going to go and see some friends.'

'Why are you going to go and see some friends?' asked John. 'I thought you were going to help me find out who killed my uncle.'

'I am going to,' replied Peter. 'When I was younger I had a lot of friends in Bristol. We used to meet a lot and sometimes we did stupid things.'

'What do you mean? Stupid things?' John didn't understand.

'Oh, fighting, breaking windows, borrowing cars . . .' explained Peter.

John interrupted. 'Borrowing cars?'

Peter smiled. 'Well, taking them for an evening, driving around, and then leaving them.'

'Did you do that?' asked John, looking surprised.

'We had nothing else to do,' Peter continued. 'It was fun for a time.'

'Not for the people whose cars you took,' John added.

'That's true,' Peter agreed. 'Anyway, after a while I stopped seeing those friends.'

'Why?' asked John.

'Because they started stealing cars and selling them,' explained Peter.

John nodded his head. 'I understand.'

Peter went on. 'Soon after that they were caught by the police.'

'What did the police do?' asked John.

'They sent my friends to prison,' said Peter.

John looked at Peter. 'I'm sure that stopped them stealing.'

'Not really,' said Peter shaking his head, 'because in prison they met older men who taught them a lot about stealing.'

'What happened when they left prison?' inquired John.

'They came to live in Manchester,' answered Peter, 'and I'm afraid that they've continued to steal things.'

'But how does this help me?' asked John.

'When I've finished unloading the lorry, I'm going to try to find some of these old friends,' said Peter. 'As they've been in prison they know lots of criminals, lots of people who make a living[11] by stealing. Criminals always talk to each other about things like your uncle's murder. My friends may have heard something about it. Something which the police may not know.'

John smiled. 'I understand now,' he said. 'They may be able to tell us something useful – something to help us find out who killed my uncle.'

Peter stopped the lorry outside the shop where he was going to unload the biscuits.

'Right,' said Peter. 'Look, we're here now. Why don't you go to a café or the cinema – the police won't be looking for you in Manchester. I'll meet you here outside the shop at ten o'clock.'

'Can't I come with you?' asked John.

'No,' Peter replied. 'My friends might not want to talk in front of you because they don't know you.'

'OK,' said John, 'see you at ten o'clock. Thanks so much for all your help.'

'You can thank me after we've found the murderer,' said Peter.

Peter and John jumped out of the lorry. John walked off down the street and Peter went into the shop where he had to unload the biscuits. He helped the men from the shop to carry the biscuits into the back of the shop and counted all the boxes. Then he got the manager to sign the papers to show that the shop had received all the boxes. By this time it was half past six.

Peter knew he had to hurry if he was going to help John. He parked the lorry on a piece of open ground and started walking. He walked quickly with his hands in his pockets and had soon left the shopping streets behind him.

It was already getting dark and the street lights were on. Peter crossed a busy main road and continued walking as fast as he could. The houses here were smaller and older. The roads were narrower and children were playing under the street lights. Here and there, Peter could see small areas of open ground covered with broken bottles, old cars and empty tins.

Peter hurried on and soon came to a café on the corner of one of the streets. The sign outside said "Cosy Café". Peter looked in the window and then went in. He asked for a cup of tea and sat down. The café was almost empty. An ᴜ man sat in one corner reading a newspaper. At the next table to Peter sat a man of about twenty-five, smoking a cigarette. Peter drank some tea and then went over to talk to the owner of the café who was washing up dirty cups and saucers.

'Good evening,' said Peter.

'Yes,' the café owner replied. 'What can I do for you?'

'I'm looking for an old friend,' said Peter. 'He used to live near here.'

'Oh, yes, I might know him,' said the café owner, without looking up from his washing up. 'What's his name?'

'Jeff. Jeff Beck,' said Peter quietly.

The café owner dropped the cup he was holding. It broke on the floor.

'No, mister,' said the café owner. 'I don't know anyone of that name. You must have made a mistake.'

'Are you sure?' asked Peter going up close to the café owner. 'I think you do know him.'

'Look. I said I didn't. I don't like people asking questions. Why don't you go and ask someone else?' the café owner shouted. 'Go on. Get out.'

'OK,' said Peter, 'thank you for your help.'

Peter left the café and started to walk along the street.

'Excuse me, can you tell me the time?' said a voice from behind.

Peter turned round. It was the man who had been sitting next to him in the café.

'Of course,' said Peter, and looked at his watch. As he did so the man caught hold of Peter's hair and twisted his head back. Peter felt the cold steel of a knife against his throat.

'Now we're going to see whether you really do know Jeff or whether you're from the police,' the man said.

⁄isit to the Cinema

When John got out of the lorry he watched Peter go into the shop. Then John started to walk slowly along the pavement. He had never been to Manchester before and he didn't know where to go or what to do. People pushed past him as they hurried home from work. Everyone had somewhere to go or something to do, except him. He started looking in the shop windows so that people wouldn't see that he was lonely.

After a while he came to a cinema.

John went up to the cinema and looked at the photographs outside. There was a cowboy film showing. John noticed that there were other people standing looking at the photographs. If I stand here, he thought, no one will notice me. They'll think I'm waiting to go to the cinema or to meet someone.

Soon he had looked at all the photographs several times, so he stood watching the people go past. There were several other people standing outside the cinema as well – a man wearing a suit, who kept on looking at his watch, a small group of girls who were laughing together, a girl of about sixteen who seemed worried about something, a mother with two small children and lots of parcels, two boys of about John's age, smoking cigarettes and trying to look very grown-up, and an old man with a long coat.

More people came and waited for a while and then went into the cinema. A small, fat man came hurrying up to the woman with the children, kissed her, and picked up one of the children. The woman picked up the other child, and with parcels and children in their arms they rushed off together.

The group of girls finally decided to go into the cinema. A taxi stopped and a pretty girl came running up to the man in the suit who had been looking at his watch. She said she was sorry she was late and they went off happily together in the taxi.

The two boys put out their cigarettes and went into the cinema. The old man walked off down the street slowly, looking in all the shop windows. The only people left waiting outside the cinema were John and the girl who was looking worried. John looked at the clock outside the cinema entrance. It was seven-thirty. The film had started at seven-fifteen.

John looked at the girl. She was thin, quite tall and had short, brown hair. She looked about the same age as John. She was walking up and down with an angry look on her face.

She looks quite nice, thought John. I wonder what she would do if I asked her to go to the cinema with me. I expect she's waiting for someone. But she's been waiting for a long time now. Perhaps the person she's waiting for isn't going to come. Shall I go and ask her to go into the cinema with me? What if she laughs at me? What if she calls a policeman?

As he was thinking this, John looked up. To his surprise, he saw that the girl was not the only other person there. There was a man standing outside the cinema as well. A policeman.

John stood quite still. He wasn't sure what to do. If he walked away, perhaps the policeman would stop him and ask him questions. If he stood there, perhaps the policeman would ask him why he was waiting.

The policeman looked at John. John looked away and pretended to look at the photographs. After a minute, John looked back at the policeman. He was still staring at him. Then the policeman started to walk towards him.

Well, John thought, there's only one thing to do now. I must talk to the girl so that the policeman will think I live here.

John walked up to the girl and said, 'Hello'.

'Hello,' the girl said in reply.

There was a silence.

'Do you want to go in and see the film with me?' John asked suddenly.

'I don't know,' the girl replied, looking surprised. 'I'm waiting for my boyfriend. But I've been waiting for half an hour and he hasn't come yet.'

'Perhaps he won't come,' said John quickly. 'Perhaps he has taken another girl to the cinema instead.'

The girl smiled. 'Well, if he's done that,' she said, 'I'll come in with you. But he may just be late and he'll be angry if he gets here and doesn't find me.'

The policeman came closer.

John took hold of the girl's hand. 'Come on,' he said to her, 'the film's already started.'

'All right, then,' the girl replied, 'but I hope Steve doesn't get angry.'

'Who's Steve?' asked John.

'My boyfriend,' she replied, as they went up to buy tickets.

'Oh, don't worry about him,' said John, feeling very happy because he had escaped from the policeman. 'Your boyfriend will never know you went into the cinema with me, will he?'

John turned to the ticket office and asked for two seats at the back.

'Do you want to go in and see the film with me?'

'That's six pounds sixty, please,' said the woman selling the tickets.

John gave her the money. 'What's your name?' he asked, turning to the girl.

'Susan,' she replied. 'What's your name?'

'John,' he said with a smile. He took her hand and they went into the cinema together. The film had already started and it was dark inside. They found two seats at the back and sat down.

Susan squeezed John's hand. 'I like you,' she said to him. 'You're nice.'

6

The Cabaret Club

The man holding the knife pushed Peter and said, 'Come on.'
'All right,' said Peter, 'I'll go with you. Jeff's a friend of mine and he'll be angry with you if you hurt me.'

'Come on then,' repeated the man, 'let's go.'

They walked along the dark street. The man with the knife walked just behind Peter. At the corner a big car was parked.

'Stop here,' the man said, and opened the door of the car. 'Get in. Don't try to escape or do anything stupid.'

The man started the engine and drove very fast through the narrow, dark streets. After only five minutes, the car stopped outside a big house. There was a sign outside the house which said "Cabaret Club". There were lots of cars parked in front of the house.

'Get out,' the man said. Peter got out of the car and stood on the pavement.

'This way,' said the man, pushing Peter towards the front door. Peter could hear music coming from the house. The man rang the bell and a little window in the door opened. A man's face appeared in the window.

'What do you want?' asked the face.

'It's me,' said the man from the café. 'I've brought someone who says that he's a friend of Jeff.'

'Jeff's in the back room,' the man at the door replied and opened the door to let them in. The man from the café took Peter through the hall and stopped outside a door at the end of the corridor. Peter looked around. The rooms on each side of the hall were full of people drinking, talking and playing cards. The man with Peter knocked at the door and pushed Peter into the room.

It was a small room, full of smoke. Three men were sitting around a table playing cards. One of the men turned around and looked at Peter. It was Jeff.

'Well, look who has come to visit us,' Jeff said in a surprised voice. Then Jeff turned to the man who had brought Peter from the café and asked, 'Why did you bring Peter here?'

'Well, boss,' the man replied, 'he said he was a friend of yours, but I thought he was from the police.'

'Well, you're wrong,' said Jeff. 'Peter is a friend of mine and I hope you didn't hurt him.'

Peter smiled because he was pleased that Jeff remembered him.

'OK,' said Jeff, 'all of you get out. I want to talk to my old friend, Peter.'

The others left the room and Peter and Jeff were alone.

'Well, Jeff,' said Peter, sitting down. 'You haven't changed much.'

'Perhaps not,' replied Jeff, 'but I'm much richer now. I own this club.'

Peter grinned. 'So you've stopped stealing and started working honestly.'

Jeff laughed. 'Well, not exactly. You could say that I control the people who do the stealing. I sell the things which they steal.

The club makes it very easy for me to do this because lots of people come here every day.'

'Anyway,' Peter said, 'I didn't come here for lessons about being a successful criminal. I need your help.'

'Why?' asked Jeff.

Peter told Jeff the whole story – that Peter had given John a lift, that the police thought that John had killed his uncle, but that John said that he hadn't killed him.

'I don't think John did kill his uncle Peter continued, ' but how can we prove it?'

'There is only one way,' replied Jeff. 'You'll have to find the murderer.'

'But I don't know how to start. Have you heard anyone talking about the murder?' Peter asked.

'No,' answered Jeff, 'but if you can wait for a few minutes, I'll go and ask some of my friends if they know anything about it. Make yourself at home[12] while you are waiting.'

After Jeff had left, Peter got up and went out into the hall. He looked into the big room where the music was coming from. A man was singing, some girls were dancing and people were talking and laughing. It was quite dark and very hot.

Peter felt thirsty. He asked for a drink and a waiter brought it. Peter tried to pay for the drink, but the waiter refused to take the money.

'You're a friend of Jeff's,' the waiter said, 'so you don't have to pay.'

Ten minutes later, Jeff came back. 'Well,' he said as he sat down, 'I think I have some useful information.'

Peter nodded. 'What is it?' he asked. 'Do you know who the murderer is?'

Jeff laughed. 'Of course not,' he said. 'But I can give you the name of someone in Bristol who may be able to help you.'

'What's his name?' Peter asked.

'Bob Steel. He's a friend of mine. Bob lives by the river. He knows more about what happens in Bristol than the police do.'

'Thank you very much,' said Peter.

Jeff gave Peter a piece of paper. 'Here's Bob's address,' he said, 'and a note to say that you're a friend of mine. Bob will help you find the murderer.'

Peter stood up. 'Thank you again, but I must go now,' he said to Jeff. 'I must get back to Bristol as soon as possible.'

'Right,' replied Jeff. 'It was nice to see you again. And if you ever want another job, come and see me.'

'No, thank you,' said Peter, with a laugh. 'I don't think I'd be a very good thief.'

Jeff walked out to the door with Peter and told the man at the door to drive Peter back to his lorry in the big car.

Peter got into the car and the car drove off fast down the street.

7

John Learns a Lesson

Meanwhile, John and Susan were sitting in the cinema. They were sitting close together and John had his arm around Susan. The film wasn't very good but they were both enjoying it.

Then the film stopped and the lights came on. It was the interval[13]. John turned to Susan and said, 'I'm very thirsty. Would you like a cola?'

'Yes, please,' she replied.

John stood up. 'Stay here,' he said, 'and I'll go and get you one.'

John walked to the end of the row of seats where they were

31

sitting and up to the girl who was selling drinks and ice-creams.

'Yes, what do you want?' asked the girl with a smile.

'Two colas, please,' replied John.

'There you are. That's one pound twenty, please,' the girl said.

John gave the money to the girl and started to walk back to Susan. Then he stopped. He could see that Susan was talking to another boy. She was arguing with him. The boy seemed very angry. John heard Susan say to the boy, 'It's your own fault. You were late. Now go away and leave me alone.'

The boy didn't reply. He turned around and walked towards John. The boy bumped into John, knocking one of the bottles of cola on the ground.

'Hey, what do you think you're doing?' said John angrily.

'You had better leave my girl alone,' answered the boy, 'or I'll do more than just push you.'

John picked up the bottle from the floor and went back to Susan.

'Who was that?' John asked Susan.

'It was my boyfriend, Steve,' Susan replied. 'He's angry with me because I didn't wait for him outside the cinema.'

'What did your boyfriend say?' John asked, as he passed Susan one of the bottles.

Susan had a drink. 'Steve told me to come and sit with him,' she said.

John nodded. 'And what did you say?' he asked.

'I told Steve to go away and leave us alone. I told Steve that I was a free person and didn't belong to him. I said that he didn't own me and that I can do what I like. And anyway,' she added, 'I like you much more than him.'

John smiled. 'I certainly like you much more than I like Steve,' he said.

Just then, the lights went out and the film started again. John put his arm around Susan. 'Give me a kiss,' he whispered to her.

She did. 'Please be careful,' she whispered suddenly. 'If Steve sees us, he'll be very angry.'

John looked around just in time to see Steve walking out of the door at the back of the cinema.

'It's all right,' said John, 'Steve has just left.'

Time passed very quickly for John and Susan and soon the film finished and the lights came on.

'Look,' John said, as they waited to leave the cinema. 'I can't explain now, but I've got to go back to Bristol. If you give me your address, I'll write to you.'

When they got outside, Susan opened her bag, wrote down her address and gave it to John. While she was writing, John looked at his watch. It was quarter past ten. But he had promised to meet Peter at ten o'clock.

'I must go now, Susan,' John said. 'I'll write to you.'

'Goodbye,' Susan said, 'and take care of yourself.'

John gave her a quick kiss and started to walk back to the shop where he had said he would meet Peter. He walked quickly, thinking of Susan and the cinema.

Suddenly a voice shouted, 'Hey, you!'

John stopped and turned around. It was Susan's boyfriend, Steve.

'Where do you think you're going?' Steve said loudly.

'It's nothing to do with you,' replied John and carried on walking.

'Oh, yes it is,' shouted Steve.

John could hear feet running up behind him. He didn't turn around. Suddenly, John felt a kick on the back of the leg. He tried to run, but fell over instead. He lay on the ground and as he looked up, he saw that Steve was standing over him.

'Now we'll have a little talk,' said Steve.

'No, we won't,' said John, jumping up and pushing Steve away. Then John looked around. Steve wasn't alone. He had three friends with him.

He lay on the ground and as he looked up, he saw that Steve was standing over him.

Steve came up to John and pushed him against the wall. 'So,' he said, 'you . . . want . . . to . . . fight . . . do . . . you?' As he said each word, he pushed John hard against the wall with his hand.

John felt lost. What could he do? There were four people against him and he was in a strange town.

'We're going to teach you a lesson[14],' said Steve, with a nasty laugh. 'We're going to teach you not to try to steal my girlfriend.'

John began to feel afraid. He knew that he must do something quickly. Suddenly, he hit Steve in the stomach and tried to run away, but the other three boys caught him.

'So you're frightened, are you?' asked one of the boys.

'You can't get away now,' said another.

'We're going to teach you a lesson,' said the third.

Then one of the boys hit John hard in the face and another boy hit him in the stomach. John fell on the ground. He felt sick. Then Steve came up and started to kick him.

John was going to scream when he suddenly heard a voice which he recognised.

'Leave him alone,' said the voice. It was Peter.

8

River Street

'Leave him alone!' Peter shouted.

Steve stopped kicking John and turned around. 'Who are you?' Steve asked. 'And what do you want? Go away and mind your own business[15].'

'No, I won't mind my own business,' said Peter and hit Steve hard, knocking him back against the wall. John, seeing that the others were watching Steve and Peter fight, jumped up and started to run.

'This way,' shouted Peter. 'Get into the car.'

John ran over to the big black car which was standing by the pavement. As John got in, he looked back to see that Peter had beaten Steve. Steve and his friends were running away.

'How did you know I was here?' John asked Peter when he got into the car.

'We'll talk about it later,' said Peter.

John and Peter sat in silence until the car stopped beside Peter's lorry. Peter thanked the driver and both Peter and John got into the lorry. Peter started the engine and they drove back to Bristol.

'Now,' said Peter, as they were leaving Manchester, 'tell me how you got into the fight.'

John explained to Peter about the cinema, Susan and Steve.

'I hope that fight taught you a lesson,' said Peter, 'don't . . .'

'Yes, I know,' replied John with a laugh. 'Don't steal other boys' girlfriends. You sound just like Steve. But how did you know where I was? You arrived just in time.'

'I didn't know where you were,' replied Peter. 'It was just luck. I was in the car on the way back to the lorry when I saw the fight. I asked the driver to stop because it didn't seem to be a fair fight. It was four against one. I didn't recognise you until after I had shouted "Stop".'

'That was lucky,' said John.

'Yes,' laughed Peter. 'But next time be more careful. Next time you get into a fight I may not be there to rescue you.'

'All right,' answered John. 'But what happened when you went to see your friends? Were they able to help us?'

Peter told John about his visit to the café, the meeting with the man with the knife, and the talk with Jeff at the Cabaret Club.

'When can we go and see this man in Bristol? The one Jeff told you about,' asked John.

'It depends on when we get back to Bristol,' said Peter. 'What's the time?'

'It's eleven o'clock,' John replied.

'Well,' said Peter, 'we should arrive in Bristol at about five o'clock in the morning. If we have some sleep after we arrive, we could go and see Bob Steel before lunch.'

'Won't you have to work tomorrow?' inquired John.

Peter shook his head. 'No,' he said. 'Universal Transport don't expect me to drive back until tomorrow. So I needn't go to work tomorrow. We'll have all day tomorrow to find the murderer.'

It was warm in the lorry. John was tired after his day's excitement, so he soon went to sleep. Peter drove on and on through the night. Halfway to Bristol they stopped at a café and had coffee and some sandwiches. Then they drove on again. The big lorry was empty and so went faster than usual. There were no cars and only a few lorries on the road. They drove faster than Peter had expected and it was still dark when they arrived in Bristol.

'Wake up,' shouted Peter. 'We're in Bristol now.'

John looked out of the window sleepily.

Peter stopped the lorry. 'You had better come to Bridgwater with me,' he said. 'It may not be safe for you to stay in Bristol.'

'No, don't be stupid,' replied John. 'I can look after myself.'

'All right,' said Peter, with a smile. 'Do you want to get out here?'

'See you at lunch-time,' said John, as he got out of the lorry.

But before Peter had time to reply, John jumped back into the lorry. 'Perhaps you're right,' John said. 'I'll come to Bridgwater with you.'

'Why did you change your mind[16] so suddenly?' asked Peter.

'Because I saw two policemen walking up as I was getting out of the lorry,' answered John.

John stayed with Peter in Bridgwater. After their tiring night, they both slept well. Peter's mother was surprised to see John, but Peter explained that he was a friend in trouble. He did not explain what the trouble was. Soon after twelve o'clock the next day, they drove back into Bristol. Peter stopped the lorry outside a house close to the river. 'I think this is it,' he said. He took out the piece of paper which Jeff had given him and looked at the address.

'Bob Steel, 12 River Street. Yes, that's right.'

Number twelve River Street was a small, low house which hadn't been painted for a long time. The windows were dirty and the curtains were drawn. The house looked empty.

Peter knocked at the door. There was no answer. Peter knocked again. 'I'm coming,' shouted a voice. After a couple of minutes, the door opened a few centimetres.

'Who is it?' a voice asked.

'We want to talk to Bob Steel,' Peter replied.

'Why?' asked the voice.

'We want some information,' answered Peter.

'Come in then,' the voice said. 'You've come to the right place if you want information.'

9

Information

'Come in,' said the man at the door. He was Bob Steel. John and Peter went into the hall. It was dark and they couldn't see very much. Bob Steel went on ahead of them up the stairs.

'It smells bad here, doesn't it?' John whispered to Peter.

Peter nodded and they followed Bob Steel up the stairs and into a small room at the back of the house. Although it was the middle of the day, the curtains were drawn in this room too. The only light came from a small lamp on the table by the bed. The bed was untidy and the sheets were very dirty. The floor of the room was covered in old newspapers.

'Sit down,' said Bob Steel.

Peter and John sat down and were able to look at Bob Steel in the light for the first time. He was middle-aged and quite short. His hair was red and he had a small, red beard. He was wearing old clothes, but had a big, new gold watch on his wrist.

'I'm Bob Steel,' the man said. 'If you want information, you've come to the right person.'

'We want some information about a murder,' said Peter quietly.

'Murder?' repeated Bob Steel. 'Which murder?'

'It was my . . .' said John quickly.

'Wait a minute,' Peter said to John. 'Let me do the talking.' Then Peter turned back to Bob Steel.

'We want some information about the murder of a teacher called Stevens. He was killed the night before last.'

'Yes,' said Bob Steel and then stopped. He looked closely at John. 'I've seen your photograph in the newspaper. Aren't you the boy the police are looking for?' Bob Steel asked.

'Listen,' Peter interrupted. 'We came here to ask questions, not to answer them.'

'OK,' replied Bob Steel. 'If you give me a couple of hours, I can find out all you want to know. All I've heard about the murder so far is that Mr Stevens wasn't killed for money. There must have been some other reason.'

'That's not much help,' said Peter.

'Look,' said Bob Steel, 'I can find out a lot more but you must give me a little time. Come back after lunch and bring the money.'

'What money?' exclaimed Peter. 'Jeff Beck told us you would help us because you were a friend of his.'

'Jeff was right,' replied Bob Steel. 'I will help you, but I want a hundred pounds for helping you.'

Peter stood up. 'We'll come back at two o'clock,' he said. 'Come on, John, let's go.'

Peter and John left the house and walked down the street. They stopped at a café on the corner and went in.

'I don't know,' said John after they had sat down. 'Bob Steel wasn't much help, was he?'

'Let's wait and see,' said Peter.

'But Peter,' replied John, 'I haven't got a hundred pounds to give to Bob Steel.'

'Neither have I,' said Peter. 'I've only got twenty pounds on me.'

John laughed. 'I hope that's enough,' he said.

'It will have to be enough,' said Peter.

'But do you trust Bob Steel?' asked John. 'Do you believe that he will tell us the truth?'

'We don't have any choice,' Peter said slowly. 'We must trust him because he's the only person who can help us.'

Peter and John had lunch in the café and afterwards went back to River Street. Bob Steel was waiting for them. He took them upstairs to the same room.

'Right,' said Bob Steel when they had sat down. 'Have you got the money?'

Peter nodded. 'Have you got the information?' he asked.

Bob Steel smiled. 'I'll tell you what I've heard. Mr Stevens wasn't killed for money. He was killed by someone who knew him. He was killed by someone young.'

John went red in the face and stood up. 'What do you mean by that?' he shouted.

'Be quiet,' said Peter, 'and let Bob Steel finish.'

John sat down and stared at Bob Steel.

'He was killed by someone young,' Bob Steel repeated. 'He was killed by a boy who knew him.'

'Is that all?' asked Peter.

'Yes,' replied Bob Steel. 'Now give me the money.'

John went red in the face and stood up.

'Wait a minute,' said Peter firmly. 'I'll give you the money when you tell me the name of the murderer.'

'Give me the money now,' said Bob Steel loudly.

'Don't give him anything,' shouted John. 'He's a liar. He's not telling the truth. He wants you to think that I'm the murderer.'

Bob Steel turned and went up to John angrily. 'Listen, my boy,' he said. 'You'd better keep quiet unless you want the police to know where you are.'

'You can't frighten me,' replied John.

Bob Steel turned back to Peter. 'Now give me the money and get out,' he said.

'I tell you what I'll do,' said Peter quietly. 'I'll give you twenty pounds now and I'll give you the rest when you tell me the name of the murderer.'

Bob Steel was quiet for a minute. He looked at John and thought for a moment. He took the money. Then he smiled.

'OK,' said Bob Steel. 'Let's arrange a place to meet. How about under the clock at the railway station at half past three? I'll be able to tell you the name then.'

'We'll see you then,' said Peter. Peter and John went out together. When they were in the street, Peter turned angrily to John.

'Why don't you keep quiet?' Peter said, turning to John. 'Bob Steel is our only chance. You shouldn't shout at him or call him a liar.'

'I don't like him,' replied John. 'And anyway, he was trying to make you think that I am the murderer.'

'We'll find out who is the murderer at half past three,' said Peter and they walked off down the street.

Bob Steel watched John and Peter from his window. He waited until they had gone. Then he went downstairs and over to the public telephone box across the street. He dialled a number.

'Hello,' he said, 'is that the police?'

10

John is Arrested

'I must go to the post office,' said Peter, as he and John walked away from Bob Steel's house.

'Why?' asked John.

'I must get the eighty pounds to pay Bob Steel,' replied Peter.

'I see,' said John, 'but do you think Bob Steel will meet us at the station at half past three?'

'I expect he will,' said Peter, 'unless you made him too angry. Do you want to come to the post office with me?'

'No, thanks,' answered John, 'I can look after myself. I'll go straight to the railway station and meet you there.'

'All right,' said Peter, 'do as you like. See you at the station at half past three.'

'See you then,' said John. Then John walked off down the road towards the river. He watched the ships unloading for a while. Then he walked back up the hill towards the station. He went into the station and sat on a seat. There were lots of people in the station and no one noticed him. He watched the trains come and go. The time passed quickly, and looking at the station clock, John saw to his surprise that it was already half past three. He couldn't see either Peter or Bob Steel. John got up and walked over to the clock. Five minutes passed. He began to wonder what had happened. Suddenly, two men walked up to him.

I wonder what they want, thought John. Perhaps they want to ask the way.

'John Stevens,' the first man said. 'I am Detective Inspector Shaw. You are under arrest[17] for the murder of your uncle.'

They were policemen. John looked around to see if he could escape, but the second policeman put his hand on John's shoulder.

'Don't try to run away,' said the policeman. 'You'd better come with us.'

The policemen took John outside the railway station, where there was a police car waiting. They put John into the back seat and Detective Inspector Shaw got in beside him. The other policeman got into the driving seat and started the car. As they were driving off, John looked back at the station and saw Peter looking at the car.

'Why did you do it?' asked Detective Inspector Shaw.

'Do what?' replied John.

'Kill your uncle,' said Inspector Shaw.

'I didn't kill my uncle,' said John angrily.

'Oh yes you did,' said Inspector Shaw, looking closely at John. 'We know you did.'

John did not reply. When the police car arrived at the police station, the policemen took John inside. They put him in a small room with no window and told him to wait there.

There was no chair and John was soon tired of standing, so he sat down on the floor. A few minutes later, Inspector Shaw came in. He saw John sitting on the floor and told him to stand up. John stood up.

'Are you going to tell us all about the murder now?' asked Inspector Shaw roughly.

John didn't reply. He looked at the floor.

'Look at me, boy!' shouted the policeman.

John looked up.

'Now tell me the truth,' said Inspector Shaw. 'Tell me why you killed your uncle.'

'I didn't . . .' started John.

'I see,' interrupted Inspector Shaw. 'So you want to be difficult, do you?'

Inspector Shaw went out of the room and banged the door. John sat down again, but as soon as he did so the door opened and he was told to stand up. After about an hour another policeman came in, smiled and said hello to John.

'I'm Sergeant Black,' he said. 'Are you John?'

'Yes,' John replied.

Sergeant Black brought two chairs and he and John sat down.

'I expect you're thirsty,' said Sergeant Black. 'Would you like a cup of tea?'

'Yes, please,' said John, with a smile. He liked this policeman much more than Inspector Shaw.

Sergeant Black brought in two cups of tea and a plate of cakes.

'Now then,' said Sergeant Black kindly, 'what's all this about?'

John didn't reply.

'You can trust me,' said Sergeant Black. 'I'll understand.'

John liked Sergeant Black and he liked the tea so he started to answer the sergeant's questions.

'Did you like your uncle?' asked the sergeant.

'No,' said John slowly. 'Not very much.'

'Where have you been for the last two days?' asked Sergeant Black.

'I've been to . . .' John stopped.

Just then, there was a knock at the door. Sergeant Black got up and went out. John sat and thought for a minute. I must be more careful, he thought. I nearly said that I had been to Manchester. That would get Peter into trouble for helping me. Sergeant Black still hadn't come back, but John could hear his voice. He went up to the door and listened. Sergeant Black was talking to Inspector Shaw.

'He's starting to talk now,' said Sergeant Black.

'Good,' replied Inspector Shaw. 'He'll tell you everything now.'

John went back to his chair and sat down. That was lucky, he thought. It had all been a trick to make him talk. Sergeant Black and Inspector Shaw were working together. Sergeant Black came back into the room.

'Now,' he said, with a smile, 'where were we? Oh yes, you were just telling me that you had been to . . . I don't remember now. Where was it you said you had been?'

'I haven't been anywhere,' said John. 'And I'm not telling you anything.'

'Now, don't be stupid,' said Sergeant Black. 'If you didn't kill your uncle, you haven't got anything to be afraid of, have you? Tell me all about it and I'll see if I can help you.'

John said nothing. Sergeant Black tried asking more questions, but John didn't reply. After a while, the sergeant put John in another room with a bed and locked the door.

'Can I have some food, please?' John asked.

'Yes,' the policeman replied. 'You can have some food when you've told us the truth.'

11

Peter Finds Bob Steel

Peter looked at the police car as it drove away from the railway station. He thought that he could see John inside the car. Peter looked again. Yes, it was John. The police had caught John at the railway station. Peter ran into the station and looked under the clock, but there was no one there.

But where was Bob Steel? Perhaps Bob Steel had already left. Or perhaps he had seen the police and run away. Or perhaps Bob Steel had told the police that John would be waiting at the station at half past three.

Peter turned around angrily and left the station. Peter went back to River Street to collect his lorry. He also wanted to talk to Bob Steel again. He wanted to find out if Bob Steel had told the police about John, and if he knew anything more about the murder.

When Peter arrived at River Street, he was still feeling very angry. Peter banged on the front door of Bob's home, but there was no answer. He waited for a moment and then banged again. There was still no answer. Peter tried to look in the front windows, but he couldn't see anything because the curtains were all closed. He went around to the back of the house and banged on the back door. There was no answer.

Right, thought Peter, if Bob Steel is at home, he'll have to go out at some time. If he's out, he'll return home in the end. So I'll wait for him.

Peter walked back to the front of the house and drove his lorry around the corner, out of sight. Then Peter went into the café on the corner where he and John had waited at lunch-time. He sat at a table at the window, from which he could watch Bob Steel's front door. It was just after four o'clock. Peter drank a cup of tea and waited.

By five o'clock, Bob Steel still had not appeared. Peter drank another cup of tea and ate some biscuits. At six o'clock he went out, bought a newspaper and returned to the café. He looked at the front page of the newspaper.

Youth Arrested for Murder

Police are still trying to find the murderer of forty-four year old schoolmaster, Robert Stevens. This afternoon the police said that Mr Stevens' nephew, John, was helping them with their enquiries.

Peter pushed the newspaper away angrily. So it was true. John was under arrest. Peter asked for another cup of tea. At half past six he decided not to wait for Bob Steel any longer. He was just leaving the café, when he suddenly stopped. He could see Bob Steel walking quickly along the street away from number twelve.

Peter decided to follow him. Bob Steel went towards the centre of the town and Peter followed him. When Bob Steel stopped to cross the road, Peter hid in a doorway. When Bob Steel looked around, Peter hid behind his newspaper.

After a few minutes, Bob Steel stopped at a bus stop. Peter waited in a shop doorway, pretending to read his newspaper. The bus came and Bob Steel got on. Peter followed and sat close to the door of the bus, so that he could watch Bob Steel without being seen. Peter wasn't sure what ticket he should buy, so he asked to go to the centre of town and hoped that Bob Steel would get off there.

Peter was right. Bob Steel got off at the bus station in the centre of the town. Here, it was easier for Peter to follow because there were more people. Soon, Bob Steel turned into a narrow side street. Peter followed him. But when Peter turned the corner, he was surprised to see that the side street was empty. Peter walked along the side street slowly and carefully, stopping every few metres to listen. Half-way down the street, he could hear voices coming from a dark shop doorway. He went close to the doorway and listened. Peter could hear Bob Steel's voice, but couldn't hear all the words. Peter could only hear some of the words Bob Steel was saying.

'. . . told you . . . trust me . . . the police . . . arrest . . . railway station . . .'

Peter moved closer, to try to hear what Bob Steel was saying. Suddenly, Peter bumped into a tin which was lying on the ground. The tin made a loud noise. Bob Steel and the person he was with stopped talking. Peter jumped back and tried to hide, but it was too late.

'There's someone there,' shouted Bob Steel, and he and the person he was talking to ran off down the street. Peter ran after them. He could see both of them clearly as they ran ahead of him. The person Bob Steel had been talking to looked quite young, about fifteen or sixteen years old. At the end of the street, Bob Steel turned to the right, and the boy he had been talking to turned to the left.

Bob Steel and the person he was talking to ran off down the street. Peter ran after them.

What shall I do? thought Peter. Which one should I follow?

He decided to run after Bob Steel. He ran as fast as he could and slowly got closer and closer to Bob Steel. Bob Steel looked over his shoulder at Peter and tried to run faster. But Peter caught up with him and took hold of his coat. Bob Steel tried to get free, but he couldn't escape. Peter caught hold of Bob Steel's arm and twisted it behind his back.

'Now,' said Peter, 'you're going to tell me the truth.'

12

More Information

'Come on,' said Peter, 'tell me the truth.'

But Bob Steel didn't say anything, so Peter twisted his arm a bit more.

'Ow!' cried Bob Steel. 'Stop it.'

'I'll stop it when you start talking,' replied Peter.

'All right,' said Bob Steel, 'but I can't talk here. Let's go back to my house and I'll tell you there.'

'I've got a better idea,' said Peter. 'We'll walk back to your house and you can tell me what you know as we walk.'

'OK,' said Bob Steel, 'but please leave go of my arm.'

Peter laughed. 'No,' he said, 'I don't want you to run away again.' Then they started walking back to River Street.

'Now,' said Peter, 'did you send the police to the railway station?'

Bob Steel shook his head. 'No,' he said, 'I didn't do it.'

Peter twisted Bob Steel's arm. 'I don't believe you,' he said. 'Why did you send the police to the station? Was it for money?'

'No,' said Bob Steel, 'they didn't give me very much . . .' Then he was silent.

'Very much what?' asked Peter quickly. 'They didn't give you very much money. So you did tell the police that John was at the station, but they didn't pay you very well.'

Bob Steel didn't reply. They both walked in silence for a moment. 'Who were you talking to?' asked Peter.

'When?' said Bob Steel.

'When I caught you,' replied Peter.

'I was talking to myself,' said Bob Steel.

'No, you weren't,' Peter said firmly. 'I saw you talking to a boy. Who was he?'

Bob Steel didn't answer. They walked on in silence again and were soon back outside number twelve River Street again.

'Open the door,' Peter told Bob Steel. 'We haven't finished our conversation yet.'

When they were sitting in the upstairs room again, Peter leant forward and started to speak seriously to Bob Steel.

'Now, let's be honest with each other. You make your living by selling information. You sold information about my friend John to the police.'

Bob Steel opened his mouth to speak, but Peter ignored him and continued.

'You sold John to the police,' said Peter. 'But the police didn't pay you very much, so someone else must have paid you as well. Someone else must have given you money to tell the police where John was. Am I right?'

Bob Steel looked at the floor and didn't reply.

Peter went on. 'I think that the person who paid you to tell the police where John was must have had a reason. I think he must have had a good reason to want to see John arrested by the police. Do you know what reason?'

Bob Steel shook his head. 'No, I don't.'

'Well, I do,' said Peter. 'I think the person who paid you money to get John arrested was the murderer. Now, tell me the name of the person who paid you. Tell me his name.'

Bob Steel looked up. 'You don't understand, mister,' he said. 'I don't tell people things. I sell information. If you want to know anything more, you'll have to pay me.'

Peter raised his hand angrily to hit Bob Steel.

'Don't hit me,' Bob Steel shouted. 'If you hit me, I won't tell you anything.'

Peter lowered his hand and smiled. 'You would sell your own mother if you could,' he said. 'All right, I'll pay you. How much do you want?'

'You promised me eighty pounds,' said Bob Steel quickly.

'That's right,' answered Peter, and he took out the money. He held the money out to Bob Steel. 'Here you are,' Peter continued. 'Tell me the name of the person who paid you to get John arrested.'

Bob Steel took the money and counted it. Then he put it in a pocket of his old coat.

'Well,' he said, 'I'm afraid I can't tell you the name.'

'What!' shouted Peter angrily.

'Wait a moment. Let me explain,' said Bob Steel. 'I can't tell you the name because I don't know it. But I can tell you two things.'

'What are they?' asked Peter.

'Firstly,' said Bob Steel slowly, 'that everything I told you this afternoon was true.'

'Tell me what you said this afternoon again,' said Peter.

'Very well,' said Bob Steel. 'I told you that Mr Stevens wasn't killed for money. He was killed by someone who knew him. He was killed by someone young.'

'What's the second thing you have to tell me?' Peter asked.

'Just this,' replied Bob Steel. 'If you go to Manor Park Secondary School you will find the answers to all your questions.'

'How will I find the murderer at Manor Park Secondary School?' asked Peter in surprise.

'Mr Stevens was a teacher there,' answered Bob Steel.

Peter stood up quickly. 'I'm going to go there now,' he said. 'But I may have some more questions to ask you – especially if I find that you haven't been telling me the truth. I think I'll tie you up to make sure that you don't go out while I'm away.'

Peter picked up a piece of rope which was lying on the floor. He tied Bob Steel to the chair in which he was sitting. Then Peter ran down the stairs and out of the house, leaving the front door partly open. Manor Park Secondary School was on the other side of Bristol. It was lucky that the lorry was around the corner. Peter got into the lorry and drove off to the school very fast.

13

In the Café

Peter stopped the lorry outside Manor Park Secondary School. Then he looked at his watch. It was already eight o'clock. The school looked dark and closed. Peter got out of the lorry and then he noticed that there was a light on in one of the rooms. Peter went over to the window and looked in. There was a man of about sixty cleaning the floor of the classroom. Peter knocked at the window and the man looked up. The man saw Peter and opened the window.

'What do you want?' the man asked.

'I'd like to have a talk with you,' Peter replied.

'I'm very busy at the moment,' the man said.

'It's about Mr Stevens,' Peter said.

'Oh,' replied the man, 'you'd better come in then and we can have a talk.'

The man was the school caretaker. He cleaned the rooms and

took care of the building. The caretaker let Peter in and they sat down in the caretaker's room together.

'What do you want to know about Mr Stevens?' asked the caretaker carefully. 'Are you from the newspapers?'

Peter shook his head. 'No,' he said, 'and I'm not from the police either. I'm a friend of Mr Stevens' nephew, John.'

'Ah, yes,' said the caretaker. 'John has been arrested by the police.'

Peter nodded. 'That's right,' he said, 'but I think the police are wrong. I don't think John killed his uncle. Did you know Mr Stevens well?'

'Yes,' replied the caretaker, as he lit a cigarette. 'I've been working here for nearly twenty years and Mr Stevens had been here for ten years.'

'What was Mr Stevens like?' asked Peter.

The caretaker thought for a moment before saying anything.

'He was always very pleasant to me,' the caretaker continued, 'but his pupils did not like him.'

'Why not?' asked Peter.

'Mr Stevens lost his temper very quickly,' said the caretaker. 'He got angry very easily. He had fixed ideas about his pupils. Once he got the idea that a particular pupil was bad, he would never change his opinion.'

'Did Mr Stevens ever hit his pupils?' asked Peter.

'I think so,' replied the caretaker, 'but it would be better for you to ask some of the boys themselves.'

'Where can I find some of them now?' asked Peter.

'A lot of the boys go to a café about a kilometre from here, close to the Scala Cinema,' the caretaker replied. 'If you go there you'll find some of Mr Stevens' pupils.'

Peter thanked the caretaker. He left the school and drove down to the café which the caretaker had told him about. The café was dark inside and the radio was playing very loudly:

'See the girl with the diamond ring
She knows how to shake that thing
Oh yes, all right,
Tell me what I say.'

A crowd of boys and girls aged fifteen or sixteen were standing by the door. Peter went up to them, said hello and then asked them if they knew Mr Stevens.

'Stevens,' said one of the boys. 'I'm glad he's dead. He was terrible.'

'Why was he terrible?' asked Peter.

'Mr Stevens used to make us look stupid. He used to make jokes about our clothes and say how stupid we were all the time,' the boy explained.

'My father's in prison,' said another boy, 'and Mr Stevens used to make jokes about it in every lesson. He used to ask me if I was going to be a thief like my father.'

'Stevens used to hit us, too,' said another boy.

'Why?' Peter asked.

'He used to hit us all the time,' the boy replied. 'He hit us if we were late, or if we didn't answer his questions correctly.'

'What was Mr Stevens like in school on the day he was killed?' Peter asked the group of boys.

'It's funny you should ask that,' said one of the boys, 'because he had a big argument in our class that day.'

'What was the argument about?' inquired Peter.

'I don't remember now,' said the boy. 'I think it was because Mr Stevens said that a boy had been rude to him. The boy said he hadn't, but Mr Stevens shouted at him, and gave him a lot of extra homework[18] to do.'

'What was the name of this boy?' asked Peter.

'I think it was Tommy Logan,' said another boy.

Peter thanked the boys for their help and asked them where he

A crowd of boys and girls aged fifteen or sixteen were standing by the door.

could find Tommy Logan.

'Tommy could be anywhere,' one of them said. 'He's got a motorbike. But he usually comes here to the café at about nine o'clock, so if you wait you'll probably see him.'

Peter went into the café, got a cup of coffee and sat down. He had been waiting for nearly half an hour when he heard a motorbike arrive outside. A dark-haired boy, wearing a leather jacket, pushed through the crowd at the door. The boy came up to Peter.

'I hear that you're asking questions about me,' he said, staring at Peter. 'What do you want?'

Peter looked at the boy in the leather jacket. Peter couldn't remember where he had seen him before. Then Peter remembered. This was the boy he had seen talking to Bob Steel.

14

The Chase

Peter looked carefully at the boy in the leather jacket.

'Sit down,' Peter said. 'Are you Tommy Logan?'

'That's right,' replied the boy. He was about sixteen, with dark hair and a thin face. He seemed nervous and his eyes were moving all the time.

'I want to ask you some questions about Mr Stevens,' Peter told the boy calmly.

'Are you from the police?' asked Tommy Logan.

Peter shook his head. 'No, I'm not,' he said.

'In that case,' replied the boy, 'I don't have to talk to you. Goodbye.'

The boy stood up and turned to go. Peter caught hold of the sleeve of the boy's leather jacket.

'Don't go yet,' Peter said quietly. 'Let's talk about your friend, Bob Steel.'

A look of fear came into Tommy Logan's eyes. He pulled his jacket out of Peter's hand and pushed his way to the door. Peter got up and ran after the boy. When Peter got to the door he was just in time to see Tommy Logan jump on his motorbike. Peter ran out on to the pavement, but it was too late. Tommy Logan started the engine and drove off.

'I know where he's going,' Peter said to himself. He ran back to his lorry and jumped in. He started the engine quickly and drove after the motorbike. But the motorbike was faster than the lorry and soon disappeared.

'Never mind,' said Peter to himself, 'I know where he's going.'

Peter drove back to River Street as fast as he could. As he turned the corner into River Street, he switched off the lorry's lights. Peter drove slowly and quietly along the street and stopped close to number twelve. Outside Bob Steel's house, Peter could see a motorbike. It was Tommy Logan's motorbike. Peter had been right in thinking that the boy would come here.

Peter climbed over the wall into the garden and went up to the front door. It was wide open. Inside, Peter could hear voices. He started to climb the stairs. Just then, the door of Bob Steel's room opened and someone switched on the light.

'There he is, on the stairs,' shouted Tommy Logan, pointing at Peter.

Before Peter could hide, Bob Steel and Tommy Logan came running out of the room. Peter got ready to stop them as they came down the stairs. Suddenly, Peter saw that Bob Steel was carrying a chair. It was the chair Peter had tied Bob Steel up in. Tommy Logan must have untied him. With a laugh, Bob Steel threw the chair at Peter from the top of the stairs. The chair was heavy. It hit Peter on the shoulder and knocked him down the stairs. Then Tommy Logan and Bob Steel ran down the stairs, jumped over Peter's body and ran out into the street.

Peter lay at the bottom of the stairs. His head and right shoulder hurt badly. Then he heard the motorbike starting. With difficulty, Peter got up and went to the door. Bob Steel and Tommy Logan were both on the motorbike and they were driving away fast down the street.

'I'm not going to lose them again,' said Peter aloud. He forgot about the pain in his shoulder and ran as fast as he could to his lorry. In a moment he was chasing after the motorbike in his lorry. The motorbike turned right at the end of the street and went down the hill towards the river. Peter switched on the lorry's headlights fully and with the tyres screaming, he followed the motorbike around the corner. Going down the hill, Peter was able to go faster than the motorbike and was soon only fifty metres behind. Then, at the bottom of the hill, the motorbike suddenly turned right into a narrow street. Peter followed the motorbike into the narrow street. As the lorry's lights lit up the wall at the end of the street, Peter shouted happily.

'Now I've got you,' he shouted. 'There's no way out!'

The street had no exit. The only way out of the street was back to the road.

The motorbike went to the end of the street, and discovering that there was no way out, turned around. Then the motorbike drove back towards Peter. Peter could see Tommy Logan's face as he drove the motorbike straight at the lorry. Peter quickly turned the lorry across the street so that the motorbike could not pass and then he waited for the crash.

With a roar, the motorbike came right up to the lorry. Then Tommy Logan saw a narrow gap between the lorry and the wall. The gap was less than a metre wide, but big enough to let

The motorbike roared through the gap between the lorry and the wall.

the motorbike escape. The motorbike roared through the gap between the lorry and the wall.

Peter was furious. Angrily, he turned the lorry around and began to chase the motorbike. When he turned into the road by the river, Peter could just see the back light of the motorbike disappearing in the distance. He drove faster. He turned a corner. And then to his surprise, Peter saw that Tommy Logan and Bob Steel had been delayed. They had stopped in a queue of cars at the traffic lights. The lights were red and so the cars had to wait.

Tommy Logan looked over his shoulder and saw that Peter's lorry was approaching fast. Peter was now very close. Tommy Logan decided that he would not wait at the red lights. Suddenly, he drove the motorbike out into the middle of the road and passed all the cars waiting at the traffic lights. Then, without stopping, the motorbike went straight across the crossroads against the red lights and nearly crashed into a car coming the other way.

Peter immediately followed the motorbike and passed the line of cars which was waiting. He didn't wait for the traffic lights to turn green. He drove faster and chased Tommy Logan and Bob Steel across the crossroads and down the street.

They were getting nearer the centre of town now and the roads were busier. As Peter passed car after car in his chase after the two men, he looked in the lorry's mirror. In the mirror, Peter could see a police car with its lights flashing, chasing both the lorry and the motorbike.

Well, thought Peter, I'm not going to stop now. I'll catch that motorbike if it's the last thing I do. With the tyres screaming and smoking as they went around the corners, Peter drove his lorry as fast as he could after the motorbike. And behind both the lorry and the motorbike came the police car with its flashing lights.

15

The Police Station

At a hundred kilometres an hour, the motorbike carrying Tommy Logan and Bob Steel roared through the centre of Bristol. Peter's big lorry raced after them. Behind Peter came a police car with its blue light flashing.

Tommy Logan looked quickly over his shoulder to see if Peter was any closer. Peter was much closer. Tommy looked ahead again and saw a sign, "LOW BRIDGE AHEAD". With a smile, Tommy drove the motorbike under the bridge.

Peter saw the bridge coming, but the lorry was going too fast to stop. The lorry was quite high and Peter thought it would hit the top of the bridge and crash. With a loud roar, the lorry went under the bridge and missed the top by a few centimetres. Peter wiped the sweat from his forehead.

'That was close,' Peter said to himself.

Peter looked in the mirror again. There were now two police cars behind! He could see their blue lights flashing, but he decided he wouldn't stop. He had to drive on.

Slowly but surely, Peter got closer and closer to the motorbike. Soon he was next to it. The motorbike and the lorry screamed down the street side by side. A car coming in the opposite direction saw the lorry and motorbike and drove up onto the pavement to avoid a crash. Finally, Peter got a little in front of the motorbike and slowed down to make it stop.

Tommy Logan also slowed down. Then he suddenly drove the motorbike up onto the pavement and passed Peter again. The people on the pavement jumped for their lives[19] when they saw the motorbike coming towards them. Bob Steel's face was white with fear as he held onto Tommy Logan's back. Tommy drove the bike onto the road again. He was now fifty metres ahead of Peter.

The road was straight now for nearly a kilometre. The two police cars behind the lorry were now much closer. Peter could see the flashing lights of another police car in front of them. Tommy Logan saw the police car coming too and started to slow down. A moment later, Tommy turned the motorbike around and came roaring back towards Peter.

Peter stopped the lorry in the middle of the road. The two police cars behind the lorry screamed to a stop, one on each side of the lorry. Now there was no space for the motorbike to pass. Peter jumped out of his lorry and started running towards the motorbike. Tommy Logan drove the motorbike straight at Peter, but at the last moment Peter jumped aside. The motorbike crashed into the lorry.

Peter stood still in the middle of the road for a second. He watched the motorbike hit the back wheel of his lorry. Behind him he could hear the policemen getting out of their cars and running towards him and the motorbike. In front of him, another policeman pointed at him and shouted, 'Stop'.

Tommy Logan was not hurt. He jumped up immediately and started to run away. Peter chased after him. As he ran, Peter quickly looked behind him. Bob Steel was lying on the ground by the motorbike with a policeman standing over him. Two other policemen were chasing Peter.

Peter could run faster than Tommy Logan. He got closer and closer and finally jumped and caught Tommy by the shoulders. They both fell to the ground, with Peter holding on to Tommy's coat. Then Peter felt two strong hands pulling him away. He looked up and saw two policemen.

'All right, you two; stop fighting. You're both under arrest,' said one of the policemen.

Then Peter felt two strong hands pulling him away.

Peter and Tommy both stood up and looked at each other.

'Now, come with us,' said the policeman, who was now firmly holding Tommy's arm. And the four of them walked back to the police cars.

Another policeman was waiting for them with Bob Steel. Bob Steel had some blood on his face, but he looked more frightened than hurt. The motorbike was put in the back of Peter's lorry and a policeman drove it back to the police station. Peter, Tommy Logan and Bob Steel followed in the police cars.

When they arrived at the police station, they were taken to see the sergeant.

The sergeant took their names and addresses. 'Now then,' he said, 'what's all this about?'

Bob Steel and Tommy Logan said nothing.

Peter thought for a minute and then he spoke. 'It's about the murder. The murder of Mr Stevens.'

'Really?' said the sergeant. 'You were driving through Bristol at a hundred kilometres an hour because Mr Stevens was murdered, were you?'

Peter tried to explain the situation, but the sergeant didn't want to listen.

'If it's about the murder,' the sergeant said, 'you can talk to the Inspector. He's out now, but he'll be back in half an hour. I hope you're telling the truth, because the inspector is a very busy man. He'll be very angry if he thinks you're wasting his time.'

'He's mad,' shouted Bob Steel, pointing at Peter.

'All right, be quiet, all of you,' said the sergeant. 'You can all talk to the inspector when he comes.'

The sergeant took Bob Steel and Tommy Logan and put them in one room. Then he opened another door and pushed Peter into a different room.

'Peter!' shouted a voice.

Peter looked up. It was John.

'Peter, how good to see you. Is everything all right now?'

asked John. 'Are they going to let me go?'

'No,' said Peter sadly.

'Then what are you doing here?' asked John.

'I'm under arrest, too,' said Peter.

'What for?' John asked in surprise.

'Dangerous driving,' replied Peter. He told John the whole story and John listened without saying anything. Then John told Peter that the police had asked him lots of questions, but that he hadn't told them anything.

'I think it's about time you did tell us everything,' said a voice from behind them. It was Inspector Shaw.

'Now,' said Inspector Shaw, 'you're both in bad trouble. I want the truth.'

16

The Truth is Told

Inspector Shaw sat down. He looked at Peter and John.

'I want the truth,' the inspector said again.

Peter looked serious. He was going to tell the inspector the whole story. He hoped Inspector Shaw would believe him. If the inspector didn't believe his story, Peter knew that he would be sent to prison for helping John and for driving dangerously. Inspector Shaw listened without saying anything, while Peter told him the whole story from the moment he had given John a lift to the chase through Bristol. The inspector wrote some notes in a little book while Peter was talking.

'Do you expect me to believe this story?' asked Inspector Shaw, when Peter had finished.

'Yes,' said Peter.

'It's the truth,' John added.

'We'll see,' replied the inspector, as he left the room.

Inspector Shaw returned a minute later with Sergeant Black, Bob Steel and Tommy Logan. Sergeant Black brought in some chairs and they all sat down.

Inspector Shaw turned to Bob Steel, who looked very frightened.

'You've been in trouble before,' said the inspector, 'and this time you'll go to prison unless you tell us all that you know.'

'Prison?' said Bob Steel. 'I haven't done anything. I haven't killed anyone. I was just walking past Mr Stevens' house the night before last, when I saw . . .'

'Be quiet, you old fool,' shouted Tommy Logan, as he jumped to his feet. Sergeant Black pushed Tommy back into his chair.

'What did you see?' Inspector Shaw asked Bob Steel.

Bob Steel continued. 'I saw a young man running out of the house. He left the front door open. I was surprised, so I went in to have a look. Mr Stevens was lying on the floor.'

'Who was the boy you saw running out of the house?' asked the Inspector.

Bob Steel pointed at John. 'It was him,' he said.

'I didn't . . .' started John.

'Be quiet,' said Sergeant Black.

'What happened next?' the Inspector asked Bob Steel.

'Well,' Bob Steel continued, 'Mr Stevens was lying on the floor. I could see that he wasn't dead because he was breathing. Just then, I heard footsteps coming, so I ran out of the back door and hid in the garden. I could hear a loud argument and then a fight. I went around to the front of the house and looked in the window, but I couldn't see anything. I waited and after a few minutes I saw a young man leaving the house.'

'Was it the same boy as before?' Inspector Shaw asked.

Bob Steel looked at Tommy Logan. 'No,' he said, 'it was Tommy Logan.'

'You're a liar,' shouted Tommy Logan. 'That's not true.'

'What did you do then?' asked the inspector.

'I went into the house again,' replied Bob Steel, 'but when I saw that Mr Stevens was dead, I left. I telephoned the police and then went home.'

'That's not true,' shouted Tommy Logan. 'That's not true. Bob Steel followed me and then asked me for money. He said if I didn't give him a hundred pounds, he would tell the police he had seen me at Mr Stevens' house.'

'So you were at Mr Stevens' house,' the inspector said quickly.

'Yes, that's right,' replied Tommy Logan. He looked angry and at the same time he looked as if he was going to cry.

'Bob Steel kept on asking for more money,' said Tommy Logan. 'I gave him some more, but it was no use. You've caught me anyway.'

Tommy Logan stopped talking and started to cry.

'Stop crying,' said Inspector Shaw to Tommy roughly, 'and tell us what happened when you went to Mr Stevens' house.'

'I didn't mean to . . .' started Tommy Logan, 'I didn't mean to . . .'

'Come on,' said Inspector Shaw in a more gentle voice. 'Tell us what happened.'

Tommy Logan looked around at the others. 'I went to see Mr Stevens,' Tommy continued, 'because he had given me a lot of extra work to do. He had given me some extra homework because he thought I had been rude to him in class. I did the work at home and then took it around to Mr Stevens' house. I wanted to explain to him that I thought he was being unfair to me. When I got to the house, the front door was open. I knocked, but there was no answer. I went into the front room and I saw Mr Stevens lying on the floor. I thought he was ill, so I started to lift him up.'

'What did Mr Stevens do?' asked the Inspector.

'Mr Stevens opened his eyes and looked at me. Then he pushed me away and stood up. I gave him the work that I had done. Mr Stevens looked at it for a minute and then threw it on the floor. He said it was all wrong. He hit me hard on the face, and said that he was going to teach me a lesson. I told Mr Stevens that he didn't have any right to hit me. He just laughed. I tried to leave, but he stopped me. Then he took off his coat and said he was going to beat me. I pushed him away and ran for the door. But Mr Stevens got there first and pushed me back.'

Tommy Logan stopped talking and looked quickly at the inspector.

'And what happened then?' the inspector asked.

'Mr Stevens started hitting me on the head and on the body,' Tommy Logan continued.

'He was hitting me hard, so I became angry and picked up a chair to push him away. Mr Stevens caught hold of the chair and it broke. One of the legs fell on the floor, so I picked up the chair leg instead. Mr Stevens laughed and said I couldn't hurt him however hard I tried. He hit me again.

' "Come on," he said, "hit me. Are you frightened to hit me?" Then Mr Stevens came closer and hit me in the face again. I hit him with the chair leg. He stopped and picked up another chair leg. Then he shouted that he was going to kill me. He ran towards me, holding the chair leg. As he came close, I hit him with all my strength and he fell to the floor.'

Tommy Logan stopped speaking and there was a short silence. Then he looked at the inspector and at John. 'I didn't mean to do it,' he said. 'I didn't mean to do it.'

17

Another Hitch-hiker

Peter and John walked out of the police station.

'It's wonderful,' John said. 'I didn't think the police would let me go.'

'The police had to let you go,' replied Peter, 'because Tommy Logan said that he had killed your uncle.'

'I know,' said John slowly, 'but I don't think he wanted to kill my uncle. I think it was an accident.'

'That's true,' agreed Peter.

Peter and John walked around to the back of the police station and got into Peter's lorry.

'What do you think will happen to Tommy Logan?' asked John.

'I don't know,' answered Peter, as he drove the lorry out onto the road. 'He is very young to go to prison. The person who should go to prison is Bob Steel, because he tried to make money out of your uncle's death.'

'But why aren't you angry with Tommy for trying to hit you with his motorbike when you were chasing him?' John asked.

'Because I expect I would have done the same in his situation,' said Peter. 'Don't forget that Bob Steel had frightened Tommy and told him that the police would put him in prison for the rest of his life,' replied Peter.

'I don't know what I'm going to do now,' said John. 'I don't want to stay at school. I must try to find a job.'

'Why not come to Universal Transport with me,' suggested Peter, 'and see if they can give you a job?'

John looked at Peter. 'Do you think they would give me a job?' he asked.

'I expect so,' said Peter, smiling.

'I hope so,' said John. 'I would like to drive lorries from Bristol to Manchester. There is someone I would very much like to see again in Manchester.'

Peter turned and smiled at John. He knew that John was thinking about the girl called Susan who he had met outside the cinema.

'I'm afraid you can't drive a lorry until you're twenty-one,' Peter said. 'But you can get a job helping to repair lorries. That's how I started when I left school.'

'I would like that,' said John.

Peter and John drove out of Bristol to Bridgwater. John was going to stay the night at Peter's house and go to Universal Transport with Peter the next day to ask for a job. Just outside Bristol they saw someone standing by the side of the road.

'Look,' shouted John, 'it's a hitch-hiker. Will you give him a lift?'

'Of course,' replied Peter and stopped the lorry. The hitch-hiker was a boy of about sixteen.

'Where are you going?' Peter shouted through the window.

'I don't know,' answered the boy. 'I'm running away from home.'

'Oh no!' said Peter, with a laugh. 'We can take you to Bridgwater if you like.'

The boy got in and sat down. He looked very nervous.

'So you're running away from home, are you?' said John to the boy with a smile.

'I expect you think you've killed your uncle too,' Peter said to the boy.

Then John and Peter looked at each other and started laughing.

'I don't understand what you are talking about,' said the hitch-hiker. 'And why are you laughing at me?'

Peter and John were laughing too much to reply.

'Let me get out of this lorry,' shouted the hitch-hiker. 'I think you are both mad.'

Peter stopped the lorry and let the hitch-hiker out. Then Peter and John drove off towards Bridgwater. They were both still laughing.

Points for Understanding

1

1 Where did Peter live?
2 What was Peter's job?
3 Where was Peter going?
4 How old was John and what was he wearing?
5 What had John done?

2

1 Why did John hit his uncle?
2 Why did John run away?
3 What was John's full name?
4 Where did John go to sleep?
5 Who stopped Peter's lorry?

3

1 Why was Peter's lorry stopped?
2 Did John know that his uncle was dead before Peter told him?
3 Did Peter think that John had killed his uncle?
4 Peter said that he and John were going to do two things. What were they?

4

1 Why did Peter want to see his old friends?
2 Where and at what time did Peter tell John to meet him?
3 What did Peter ask the owner of the Cosy Café?
4 Was the man from the café sure that Peter was a friend of Jeff Beck?

5

1 Why did John stop outside the cinema?
2 Why did John speak to the girl?
3 Who was Steve?

6

1 Who did Peter recognise in the club?
2 How did Jeff Beck earn his living?
3 How did Jeff help Peter?
4 What was the name of Jeff's friend in Bristol?

7

1 What did John tell Susan when they left the cinema?
2 Why did John leave Susan?
3 Why did Steve and his friends hit John?
4 Who was winning the fight when John heard Peter's voice?

8

1 Why did Peter get out of the car when he saw the fight?
2 Why was Peter free to help John the next day?
3 Why did John quickly get back into the lorry?
4 Where did Peter and John go when they woke up?

9

1 Why did Peter and John go to visit Bob Steel?
2 Did Bob Steel want money for helping Peter and John?
3 Did John trust Bob Steel?
4 How did Bob Steel describe Mr Stevens' murderer?
5 Where and at what time did Bob Steel tell Peter and John to meet him?
6 Why do you think Bob Steel telephoned the police?

10

1 Why did Peter go to the post office?
2 Why did the two men at the station speak to John?
3 Where did they take John?
4 Why did Sergeant Black treat John kindly?
5 Did the policeman think that John was telling the truth?

11

1 Who did Peter see at the railway station?
2 What did Peter read in the newspaper?
3 How old was the person who was talking to Bob Steel?
4 Who did Peter chase and catch?

12

1 Did Bob Steel tell the police that John was at the railway station?
2 Peter said that the police paid Bob Steel for the information about John. Who else did Peter suggest paid Bob Steel?
3 What did Peter do to Bob Steel before he left?
4 Why did Peter go to Manor Park Secondary School?

13

1 Why didn't Mr Stevens' pupils like him?
2 Why did the caretaker tell Peter to go to the café?
3 What happened in the school on the day when Mr Stevens was killed?
4 Why did Peter want to speak to Tommy Logan?
5 Where had Peter seen Tommy Logan before?

14

1 Why did Tommy Logan run away from Peter?
2 Where did Tommy Logan go?
3 How did the traffic lights help Peter?
4 What other car was following the lorry and the motorbike?

15

1 Why were the police cars chasing the lorry and the motorbike?
2 What did Peter tell the sergeant?
3 Did the sergeant believe Peter?
4 Why was John pleased to see Peter?

16

1 Who had Bob Steel seen running out of Mr Stevens' house?
2 Was Mr Stevens alive or dead after John ran out of the house?

3 What did Bob Steel hear and see after Tommy Logan went into the house?
4 What did Bob Steel really do after he left the house?
5 Why had Tommy Logan gone to see Mr Stevens?
6 Why did Mr Stevens hit Tommy?
7 What did Mr Stevens tell Tommy to do when Tommy picked up the chair leg?
8 Who killed Mr Stevens?

17

1 Did John think that Tommy Logan wanted to kill his uncle?
2 Who did Peter think ought to go to prison?
3 What job did Peter suggest for John?
4 Who did John want to see again in Manchester?
5 Why did John and Peter start laughing?

Glossary

1 *pass a driving test* (page 4)
to succeed in a test which allows you to drive a car or a lorry on the road. In England a person cannot drive a lorry until he/she is twenty-one.

2 *goods* (page 4)
things that are being carried from one place to another place. In this story the goods are biscuits.

3 *night club* (page 5)
a place where people go in the evening to drink and dance.

4 *OK* (page 7)
all right.

5 *take care of yourself* (page 8)
look after yourself, be careful, don't do anything stupid. A person will often say 'take care of yourself' when he is saying goodbye to a friend.

6 *load* (page 8)
the goods which the lorry is carrying.

7 *load* (page 8)
to put the goods onto a lorry, car or train before it leaves.

8 *weather forecast* (page 9)
this tells you what the weather will be – if it is going to rain or if the sun is going to shine.

9 *hitch-hike* (page 9)
if you want to go from A to B, you might hitch-hike. You will stand at the side of the road and wait for a car or a lorry to stop and take you to B. A person who hitch-hikes is called a hitch-hiker.

10 *lift* (page 9)
when a lorry takes a hitch-hiker from one place to another, it is giving him a lift.

11 *make a living* (page 21)
the way someone makes his money. Peter makes a living by driving lorries for a company.

12 *make yourself at home* (page 30)
to feel comfortable and happy in a new place.

13 *interval* (page 31)
during a long film at the cinema there is an interval. The film stops and the lights in the cinema are switched on. The people in

the cinema have about ten minutes to talk and eat ice-creams,
etc. before the lights are switched off again and the film
continues.

14 *teach you a lesson* (page 35)
if a person makes you very angry, you might teach him a lesson.
You will do something to him so that he will not make you angry
again.

15 *mind your own business* (page 35)
to keep away from someone's private matters.

16 *change your mind* (page 37)
to think you will do something and later decide not to do it.

17 *under arrest* (page 43)
if a policeman asks you to go with him, you can refuse. But if the
policeman puts you under arrest, you must go with him.

18 *homework* (page 55)
work that must be done at home, after school.

19 *jump for your life* (page 62)
to jump or move in a very quick and surprised way.

Shane by Jack Schaefer
Old Mali and the Boy by D. R. Sherman
Bristol Murder by Philip Prowse
Tales of Goha by Leslie Caplan
The Smuggler by Piers Plowright
The Pearl by John Steinbeck
Things Fall Apart by Chinua Achebe
The Woman Who Disappeared by Philip Prowse
The Moon is Down by John Steinbeck
A Town Like Alice by Nevil Shute
The Queen of Death by John Milne
Walkabout by James Vance Marshall
Meet Me in Istanbul by Richard Chisholm
The Great Gatsby by F. Scott Fitzgerald
The Space Invaders by Geoffrey Matthews
My Cousin Rachel by Daphne du Maurier
I'm the King of the Castle by Susan Hill
Dracula by Bram Stoker
The Sign of Four by Sir Arthur Conan Doyle
The Speckled Band and Other Stories by Sir Arthur Conan Doyle
The Eye of the Tiger by Wilbur Smith
The Queen of Spades and Other Stories by Aleksandr Pushkin
The Diamond Hunters by Wilbur Smith
When Rain Clouds Gather by Bessie Head
Banker by Dick Francis
No Longer at Ease by Chinua Achebe
The Franchise Affair by Josephine Tey
The Case of the Lonely Lady by John Milne

For further information on the full selection of
Readers at all five levels in the series, please refer
to the Heinemann Readers catalogue.

Macmillan Heinemann English Language Teaching, Oxford

A division of macmillan Publishers Limited

Companies and representatives throughout theworld

ISBN 0 435 27219 5

Heinemann is a registered trade mark of Reed Educational and Professional Publishing Ltd

© Philip Prowse 1973, 1992
First Published 1973
Reprinted eight times
This edition published 1992

A recorded version of this story is available on cassette
ISBN 0 435 27275 6

All rights reserved; no part of this publication may be
reproduced, stored in a retrieval system, or transmitted, in any
form or by any means, electronic, mechanical, photocopying,
recording or otherwise, without the prior written permission of
the Publishers.

Illustrated by Mike Brownlow
Typography by Adrian Hodgkins
Cover by Amanda Hutt and Threefold Design
Typeset in 11/12.5 pt Goudy
by Joshua Associates Ltd, Oxford
Printed and bound in Great Britain by Cox and Wyman

98 99 00 10 9 8 7 6 5